**Puffin Books**
**Ninety-nine Dragons**

'I think sheep are soppy,' said Ben, so he used dragons instead. He had to count something, or he'd never have got to sleep at all on such a hot night. So off he went counting handsome, greedy green dragons with yellow underbellies jumping stylishly over a splendid tall gate, while his sister Beth, a good girl, counted ordinary old sheep hopping over a nice little green gate.

'Eighty-eight, eighty-nine,' counted Ben, and the sleepier he got the smaller were the dragons, until when he reached ninety-nine, there was a really tiny dragon who couldn't get over the gate at all, but fell back into the middle of his bed. Then, to Ben's dismay, the little dragon began to cry.

Whatever could he do, Ben wondered? Even if he could help the poor little thing over the gate it would never catch up with its family now, and it was all his fault because he shouldn't have made the gate so high! But worse was to come, for all the other ninety-eight ravening and carnivorous dragons were now disporting themselves in the land Over-the-Gate, the same place where Beth's fifty sweet little sheep and lambs had gone hopping so gaily. It was too awful to think of.

Could they send Ninety-nine to warn the sheep? Not with that look in his eye, they decided! He was a dragon after all, even if he was tiny. No, they would have to go over the gate and rescue the sheep themselves!

This deliciously funny, exciting and original fantasy is by the author of *Carbonel, The Kingdom of Carbonel, Carbonel and Calidor* and *Grimblegraw and the Wuthering Witch*, also published in Puffin.

Barbara Sleigh

# Ninety-nine Dragons

Illustrated by Gunvor Edwards

Puffin Books

Puffin Books, Penguin Books Ltd, Harmondsworth, Middlesex, England
Viking Penguin Inc., 40 West 23rd Street, New York, New York 10010, U.S.A.
Penguin Books Australia Ltd, Ringwood, Victoria, Australia
Penguin Books Canada Ltd, 2801 John Street, Markham, Ontario, Canada L3R 1B4
Penguin Books (N.Z.) Ltd, 182–190 Wairau Road, Auckland 10, New Zealand

First published by Hodder and Stoughton Ltd 1974
Published in Puffin Books 1977
Reprinted 1978, 1980, 1983, 1985

Made and printed in Great Britain by
Richard Clay (The Chaucer Press) Ltd, Bungay, Suffolk
Set in Monotype Garamond

# Contents

# 1. Ben and Beth

It was a small bedroom, with just enough room for a chair, a chest of drawers with a little spotty mirror hanging above it, and two beds: and, of course, for Ben and Beth who slept in them. They both had green flowery bedspreads, but Ben's had a pattern of red flowers while Beth's were blue.

They had gone to bed on one of those warm summer evenings when although the window and door were wide open, there was not a whiff of moving air to stir the curtains. All the world outside seemed to be as busy as though it was midday. A blackbird sang on a lamp-post on the other side of the street, and people laughed and talked as they passed below.

Inside, the room seemed to grow hotter and hotter, and the bedclothes more rumpled. At last Ben gave a great gusty sigh and called out:

'We can't go to sleep! We've got too many bedclothes on!'

So their mother came upstairs and took off a blanket from each bed, tucked in their sheets and tidied their flowery bedspreads and kissed them good night once more.

But it didn't make a ha'p'orth of difference. They still couldn't go to sleep.

When they had tossed about for at least ten minutes, Ben said:

'Go on, Beth! It's your turn!'

So Beth called out:

'We still can't go to sleep! We've come all untucked!'

Their mother came upstairs again, rather more slowly this time, and turned their pillows over and smoothed their beds. But still it didn't make a ha'p'orth of difference.

In five minutes they were just as un-sleepy and untucked as before. So Beth said to Ben:

'Go on! It's your turn again!'

So Ben called out:

'We can't go to sleep! We want a drink of waa-ter!'

This time their father came upstairs, two at a time, because he was watching an exciting western on television, and he wanted to get back to it again.

'All right! All right!' he said. 'I'll get you a drink of water, and then there's to be no more calling out, or you'll never get to sleep at all.'

He fetched them each a tooth mug from the bathroom brim full of water. Usually if they couldn't sleep they could manage to keep him talking for a little while, but this evening he had left the good cowboy tied up in a burning house by the bad cowboy, and he was dying to know if he would escape, so he said briskly:

'Why don't you shut your eyes tight, and count sheep jumping over a gate? That's supposed to make you sleepy.'

'I think sheep are soppy,' said Ben.

'I don't,' said Beth. 'I like sheep. Specially the kind with black faces and black stockings, and all the rest of them white and woolly.'

'Would it be the same if I counted dragons jumping over a gate instead of sheep?' asked Ben.

'I should think so,' said his father absently. 'Haven't you finished that water yet?' It was more interesting than plain water because it tasted of tooth-paste, so they were both drinking rather slowly. 'Well, I can't wait any longer. You can put your mugs down on the floor when you've finished. But don't call out any more! I shall shut the door so that we shan't hear you even if you do!'

He closed the door firmly, and Ben and Beth heard him running downstairs again. Suddenly the tooth-pasty water didn't taste nice any longer, so they bent over and put the mugs on the floor between the two beds. Unfortunately they both upset.

'Better call Dad to mop it up,' said Beth.

'Not me!' said Ben. 'Not after what he said. And anyway, now the door's shut they wouldn't hear. I should think it's so hot the water will dry up by itself by the morning.'

Beth sighed and flumped back on her pillow.

'I suppose we may as well *try* counting sheep jumping over a gate,' she said.

'Dragons!' said Ben.

'Sheep!' said Beth.

'Dragons!' said Ben.

'Oh, well, I suppose you can make it bulldozers if you like,' said Beth crossly. 'But I shall make it sheep!'

And she sat up and punched her pillow and then lay down again, with her knees drawn up in a hump under the bedclothes, which was how she always went to sleep.

## 2. The Two Gates

Ben and Beth both squeezed their eyes tight shut, and
Beth began counting white woolly sheep with black faces
and black stockings jumping over a little green gate. But
Ben started counting scaly dragons jumping over a
splendid, tall iron gate, with golden curlicues on the top,
like the one that led into the park at the end of the street.
Of course the dragons were not very big. Ben knew that
only little dragons can jump, before their wings have
grown properly. Big ones either fly, or just lollop. They
were all as green as parsley on top, and yellow as
scrambled egg underneath, with a row of nobbles down
the back that ended in a spiky tail, which bounced along
the ground as its owner scuttled up to the gate for the
take-off. Each dragon paused before it jumped, drew itself
together, blew a small flame and a couple of smoke rings
through its nostrils, clapped together the little green
flippers that one day were going to grow into great
leathery wings, and with a 'Whoops!' over the gate it
went, with the next dragon close behind.

'Sixty-one, sixty-two,' counted Ben, and then he
yawned. 'I think I'm getting sleepy!' he said to himself.
Aloud to Beth he went on: 'I say, it's a funny thing –' he
yawned again and snuggled down under the bedclothes,
'but the sleepier I grow the smaller the dragons seem to
get!'

But there was no answer from Beth. She was asleep already; the blue flowery bedspread moved very slightly up and down with her even breathing.

'Eighty-eight, eighty-nine,' counted Ben sleepily.

Now when he reached dragon ninety-eight he was almost asleep, and dragon ninety-nine was very small indeed; not much bigger than a kitten. But it clapped its flippers together bravely, as the others had done, blew a couple of sparks and a tiny thread of smoke through its nostrils, and jumped with a 'Whoops!' which was little more than a squeak. But instead of sailing over the gate as its companions had done, it stumbled against one of the golden curlicues on top of the great high gate, and fell back, plop! right on to the middle of Ben's bed, with a sad little 'Wheee!' and a slight smell of singeing.

Ben shot up in bed, very wide awake all at once. He stared at the little dragon over the hump of his knees, and the little dragon stared back, and I don't know which of them was the more surprised.

There was a long pause, and then Ben said:

'Hadn't you better go after the others?'

'How can I?' said Dragon Ninety-nine. 'That great iron gate is too high for me to jump over. They've all gone without me. Whatever shall I do?'

To Ben's horror two tears welled up from its slanting golden eyes, and trickled down its long green nose, to dry with a sizzle when they reached its smoking nostrils. 'Even if I could get over the gate I should never catch up with the others, not with my short legs. They're all bigger than me,' it went on unhappily.

Ben leaned over and shook Beth by the shoulder.

'Wake up! Wake up!' he said. 'Something awful's happened!'

'What's the matter?' said Beth, sleepily rubbing her eyes. But when she saw the little dragon she sat up at once.

'Whatever's that?' she said.

'I'm not a that, I'm a dragon!' it said sulkily, and the tears began to run down its long nose faster than ever, so that it almost disappeared in the cloud of steam they made.

'But however did it get here?' asked Beth.

'It tripped and fell on the top of my gate because it was too high for it to jump over. It was like the ones leading into the park. But never mind about that now. Whatever are we going to do with it? I mean to say – a dragon!'

'You should have counted sheep like Daddy said!' went on Beth in a rather maddening way. 'My sheep were so sweet! Especially the lambkins at the end; all of them had black stockings and black faces. My little green gate was quite easy to get over. I was fast asleep by the time I had counted fifty.'

'A little *green* gate?' said the dragon, wiping his tears with the back of a scaly paw. 'My favourite colour!' he went on, in the hiccupy way of someone who is beginning to stop crying. 'Some people have no consideration.' He looked reproachfully at Ben, then he added suddenly: 'Sheep did you say? My favourite food too.'

'What!' said Ben and Beth together with one horrified voice.

'You don't mean you'd *eat* those dear little lambs?' went on Beth.

'Given half a chance I would,' replied the dragon, and a pointed tongue flicked out and licked his lips. 'If someone gave you a box of chocolates what would you do?'

'Well, eat them of course,' said Beth. 'But that's different.'

'I don't see why,' said the dragon. 'All those dear little chocolates!' Beth didn't stop to argue. Instead she said anxiously:

'I say, Ben, however many dragons did you count?'

Ben wriggled uncomfortably. 'This one was ninety-nine.'

'Do you mean to say you've turned ninety-eight dragons loose among my fifty sheep and lambs? How could you! How simply horrible!'

'Well, you needn't talk as though I'd done it on purpose!' said Ben sullenly.

'We shall have to warn them somehow,' said Beth. 'The sheep I mean.'

'That's all very well, but how?' asked Ben.

There was silence for a moment while they thought, broken only by the occasional sizzle of one of the dragon's tears.

'Suppose we just counted Ninety-nine here,' said Beth pointing to the little dragon, 'jumping over the little green gate. Couldn't he go and warn the sheep?'

'A very good idea indeed,' said Ninety-nine. 'I'm always willing to put myself out for my friends.' But his lips curled back in a smile that Beth didn't care for at all, and his pointed tongue flicked in and out again. His tears had stopped abruptly.

'I'm pretty sure we'd better not trust him,' said Ben shortly.

'I'm pretty sure I couldn't trust myself,' said the little dragon frankly. 'So don't tempt me.'

'Then there's nothing else for it. We shall have to go and warn them ourselves!' said Beth.

'That's all very well,' said Ben. 'But how on earth . . . ?'

'How would it be if we both shut our eyes tight,' said Beth slowly. 'Yes, that's it! Then you count *me* jumping over the little green gate, and I can count *you*, at exactly the same minute! Then we could both go and warn the sheep!'

'And what about me?' said the little dragon unhappily. 'You can't leave me behind!' Once more his tears began to trickle.

'We could,' said Ben sternly, 'unless you promise faithfully not to hurt one single sheep or lamb! If you'll promise on your honour as a dragon I could carry you over when I jump. You could sit in my pyjama pocket.'

'It's not a very dragon-like place to sit,' said Ninety-nine sulkily. 'I've got my pride.'

'All right, then, you can stay behind,' said Ben shortly.

'Oh, very well, I suppose there's no help for it,' said Ninety-nine. He lifted up a claw with one talon raised and went on: 'By my scaly back and fiery breath, I swear! That's a very solemn dragon oath!'

Rather gingerly Ben picked the little creature up – he held it easily in his cupped hands – and slipped it into his pyjama pocket, where it sat with its chin and front paws on the hem, peering over the edge and blowing an occasional wisp of smoke through its nostrils. Ben gave an uncomfortable wriggle.

'Come on. Let's buck up and get this business over,' he said. 'It's like having a rather too hot hot-water bottle in your pocket. Now we'd better be quite sure what we're doing. We both close our eyes tight shut, and when I say "Ready, steady, go!" we'll call out "One!" together, very loud, as we count each other jumping over the gate. Got that!' Beth nodded.

'The little *green* gate, mind,' she said. 'Not your great tall one. I don't suppose *I* could get over that. I only hope it works!'

But it did work.

# 3. The Other Side

They screwed their eyes up very tight indeed. Beth just had time to wonder uneasily what they would find on the other side, when Ben said:

'Ready! Steady! Go!'

And as she counted one Ben jumping over the little green gate, Ben counted one Beth, and there they were, leaping up and over at exactly the same minute. They collided in mid-air, for the gate was a small one, you remember, and came down, sprawling, on the other side, on something soft.

They both opened their eyes.

They were sitting on the springy young grass of a green plain that stretched away and away into the distance, broken here and there by little hills and hummocks, rising gently to a mountain in the distance. The green gate had disappeared.

Everywhere round them the grass was thickly studded with little blue flowers. The whole scene was flooded with a light which was clearer than moonlight but softer than sunlight.

'Well,' said Beth nervously, 'here we are! What do we do now?'

'I know what I shall do!' said Ben. He hurriedly tipped the little dragon from his pyjama pocket and dropped him on the grass. He spoke jerkily, as he sucked each scorched finger in turn. 'He's twice as hot as when I picked him up – on the other side.'

'Excitement,' said Ninety-nine briefly. 'It always takes dragons like that.'

'However will you explain to Mum how you got your pocket singed when we get home again?' said Beth.

'We shall probably have a lot of explaining to do, before this lark is over!' said Ben gloomily. 'I can't think what we've done it for. There aren't any sheep or dragons to be seen anywhere.'

Ninety-nine was sitting up on his haunches so that he could see over the taller clumps of grass.

'That doesn't mean they aren't there,' he said. 'Probably gone exploring to find out what sort of place they've come to. Where the best feeding-grounds are, and where there's water. That sort of thing. And, of course, what dangers there may be.'

Beth wasn't listening.

'It's a funny thing,' she said. 'These blue flowers, I'm sure I've seen something like them before, but I can't think where.'

'Oh, cut it out!' said Ben crossly. 'Just like a girl to start drooling over flowers when Ninety-nine here says there may be dangers. What sort of dangers?' he asked.

'I don't know any more than you do,' said the little dragon. 'This over-the-gate land is Sheep Country. I don't suppose dragons have ever been here before. It's a queer

place, I've been told. But wait a minute.' He was shading his eyes with a scaly paw. 'Have a good look at that mountain!' A grin spread over his face which he quickly turned into a frown, but not before his pointed tongue had flicked out in the way that Ben remembered.

Both Ben and Beth stared hard at the mountain.

'Those white moving dots near the top!' said the dragon.

'Sheep!' said Beth excitedly. 'I'm sure they are!'

'Come on, then!' said Ben. 'What are we waiting for?'

'They look an awful long way away!' said Beth, but she reefed up her nightdress and strode out manfully.

The grass was soft to their bare feet, and they seemed to cover the ground with surprising speed, with the curious gliding motion you sometimes find in dreams, their feet barely touching the ground. The small dragon lolloped along beside them, only sometimes calling out: 'Hi! Wait for me!' Now and then he clapped his little flippers together and jumped over an extra tall clump of grass with a 'Whoops!'. Here and there Beth stooped to pick one of the blue flowers.

When they reached the foot of the mountain they could hear the distant bleating of lambs quite clearly, and the deeper baa of their mothers' answering call.

'It's the sheep all right!' said Ben, pulling up short. 'But I still can't see any dragons!'

'Then they must be somewhere else,' said Ninety-nine. 'Perhaps the other side of the mountain. They can't have discovered the sheep yet. There won't be any mistake about it when they do – because they'll all be pretty

hungry, and well – sheep; too tempting! And don't forget that I'm the littlest of them all!'

'I remember,' said Ben gloomily. 'The first dragons
over the gate were much bigger.'

Beth edged nervously up to him, and Ben looked uncomfortably over his shoulder, but still seeing no sign of
the dragons Beth said:

'Well, if they aren't here now there's no desperate
hurry, I suppose. I vote we have a bit of a breather before
we start climbing. I'm quite out of breath.'

She plumped thankfully down on the grass.

'You are a Charlie,' said Ben. 'If you hadn't kept
stopping to pick those silly blue flowers you wouldn't
have had to hurry to keep up.'

'I've got an idea about them,' said Beth.

'For heaven's sake!' said Ben. 'You and your miserable
flowers! As if –'

'Oh, do listen!' she interrupted. 'I'm sure this is important, but I don't quite know how. The blue flowers are
exactly like the ones on my bedspread! Now those were
made-up flowers, not like any real ones I've ever seen.
These here are the bedspread flowers, but *growing*, don't
you see? They've got juicy stalks that snap easily, and
leaves and buds. They've even got a queer sort of smell,
not like the smell of any other flower!'

For the first time Ben looked at the bunch his sister was
holding out to him. He stared at in silence for a minute,
and then he said slowly:

'I believe you're right,' and he fingered the soft blue
petals. 'I'm sorry I called you a Charlie.' He jumped to his
feet. 'Oh well, come on, let's get going. We can try and

think what it means while we're climbing the mountain.'

They picked themselves up and started up the slope with the same strange dream-like motion as before. But now the glide had become an upward swoop, so that the hair blew back from their hot foreheads and Beth's night-dress billowed out behind her. In no time at all they were within calling distance of the first sheep, who so far had not become aware of them, but went on contentedly cropping the grass.

'I say,' said Beth, stopping suddenly. 'Wait a minute. Wouldn't it be better if Ninety-nine stayed behind while we go ahead and do a bit of explaining? We want the sheep to know we're friends.'

'You mean if they see we've got a dragon with us they might take fright?'

Ninety-nine smirked.

'They'd probably stampede at the mere smell of me!' he said in a self-satisfied way, kneading the grass with his front paws and swishing his tiny tail from side to side.

'That's true,' said Ben. 'Silly things, sheep. They might get the wind up over even such a little dragon as Ninety-nine.'

Ninety-nine frowned in an offended way. 'Oh, very well, I know when I'm not wanted!' he said huffily.

'Of course we want you,' said Beth hurriedly. 'But please do wait here just a little while.'

'I'll whistle when we're ready for you to join us again,' went on Ben. 'Honestly.' He had just learned how to whistle down two fingers and was rather proud of it. 'Come on, Beth!'

They went on up the mountainside. Beth turned round

to see that the little dragon was not following. Only his
head and a wisp of smoke showed where they had left him
behind a clump of grass. His ears were drooping rather
wistfully and he called out a little uncertainly:

'You won't be long, will you?'

Beth waved back in what she hoped was a reassuring
way.

# 4. Father Bell-Wether

The first sheep they came to was contentedly munching grass, her broad woolly back towards them, so she did not see them coming. Ben had no idea how to address a sheep, so he cleared his throat nervously and said:

'I say, excuse me!'

The sheep turned a startled black face towards them, with a tassel of grass hanging from her mouth. She paused in her munching for a moment and then began again, gazing at them all the time with unblinking yellow eyes. When she had swallowed the last blade of grass she shook her head slowly in a puzzled way.

'Humans!' she said. 'Good gracious me, whatever next! I've jumped many a gate in my time, big 'uns and little 'uns, but I've never met a human before. Not This Side. Two of them are you?' She looked severely from Beth to Ben. 'It'll be dogs next, you mark my words!' she went on sourly. 'And then there'll be no peace for anyone, but chivvying here and chivvying there. Sheep-dogs they call them. The sort of daft name humans would think of! You're either a sheep or a dog. You can't be both. Stands to reason.'

She lowered her long face and began to nibble the grass again as though Ben and Beth were not there.

'We didn't want to come!' said Ben indignantly. 'We only did it because we thought we ought to warn you . . .'

'Warn us? Warn us, did you say? I might have known that humans This Side would bring bad luck!' The sheep let out a loud 'Ba-a-a!' looking round anxiously as she did so.

'Maatilda! Mortimer! Come here at once! Da-anger! Da-anger! Ba-a-a!'

Two very young lambs came skipping towards her, wiggling their tails, and bleating in a giggly sort of way, and a number of other sheep who had heard the call 'Danger!' left their grazing and came too. The air was full of anxious bleatings.

'What's the ma-a-a-tter?' they cried.

'Ma-a-tter?' the first sheep cried. 'You'd better ask these humans here!'

'We thought we ought to come and warn you. . .,' began Beth. She stopped as Ben nudged her rather painfully.

'Better not tell them,' he whispered. 'Too silly!' Aloud he said: 'Have you got a leader?'

'Of course we have!' came the answer from a dozen sheep. 'Father Bell-Wether!'

'Then you had better take us to him,' said Ben, 'so that we can explain.'

A large number of sheep and lambs had joined them by this time, and they set off up the last slope of the mountain, at the back of a stream of bobbing woolly backs and twinkling black legs. The air was thick with cries of: 'Da-a-anger! Huma-a-ns! Fa-a-ther Bell-Wether!' And the anxious bleatings of mother sheep calling their lambs. By the time they had reached the top of the mountain they had been joined by so many animals that Ben and Beth had to shout to one another to make themselves heard.

'I say!' said Beth suddenly. 'Look up there at that great rock, at the top!'

They both paused, while the flock of sheep hurried forward. Standing on the rock against the sky, looking down on them, was a mighty ram. He had two magnificent curling horns and round his neck was a bell.

'Father Bell-Wether!' said Beth. 'It must be!'

The flock of frightened sheep surged up the slope. When they reached the rock it divided, and flowed like water round the base. They looked up crying:

'What shall we do? What shall we do? Ba-a-a!'

The great ram flung up his head, so that the bell rang sharply at the movement, and the sheep fell silent, except for the occasional occasional bleating of a young lamb.

'What is the matter, my children?' called the ram in a deep voice.

'Humans is the matter!' came the cry.

'And warnings!'

'And dangers!'

'Humans!' said the ram in surprise. 'And what is this danger?'

'We don't know!' cried the sheep.

'Then the first thing to do is to find out!' he replied crisply.

'Make way for the humans. Perhaps they can explain.'

With much jostling the flock parted to allow Ben and Beth to pass through. When they reached the rock the two children stood at the foot and gazed up at Father Bell-Wether, a little awed by his dignity.

'You come to warn us?' he said. They both nodded. 'For that we thank you. But what is this danger?'

'Dragons!' said Ben shortly.

'Dra-a-gons! Dra-a-gons!' bleated the frightened sheep in chorus.

Father Bell-Wether stamped his hooves so that the bell rang again, and once more the flock fell silent.

'This is Sheep Country. There have never been dragons Over-the-Gate before, to my knowledge,' said the ram. 'Or humans, if it comes to that.'

'Well, they are here now,' said Ben. 'If you don't believe us we can prove it! We've brought a dragon with us, just a little one, because we couldn't leave it behind.'

He put two fingers to his lips and whistled shrilly down them: a whistle that could be heard even above the renewed bleating and shuffling of the frightened flock. 'But we made him make a solemn dragon promise that he wouldn't hurt a single sheep or lamb!' shouted Beth above the hubbub, which died down a little at this.

As she spoke they saw Ninety-nine scuttling up the slope towards them in answer to Ben's whistle, blowing puffs of smoke at every bound, his pointed tail bouncing behind him. The sheep huddled back to make an even wider path for him than they had done for Ben and Beth, and Father Bell-Wether looked down with a puzzled frown to see the little dragon rubbing himself against the children's legs like a friendly cat.

'I thought you'd forgotten me,' he said unhappily. Beth bent down and patted his scaly head, and he began to make a curious rattling noise in his throat as though he was trying to purr.

Father Bell-Wether gazed rather scornfully at the little creature.

He turned to the waiting flock of sheep.

'Go about your business, children! I do not think there is much to fear. But do not wander too far away!'

They turned obediently, and with much ba-a-ing of instructions to their lambs, went back to their munching. The first sheep the children had spoken to muttered out of the side of her mouth as she passed: 'Frightening us out of our wits for nothing!' Adding with withering scorn: 'Humans!'

'Wait, I'm coming down,' said Father Bell-Wether, when they had scattered, and he leapt lightly from the rock. 'Now we can discuss this matter in peace. Though there doesn't seem to be much danger. I think we are a match for a creature no bigger than that!' He looked sidelong at the little dragon as he spoke. 'My flock may seem foolish, but they will do as I tell them, and their hooves are sharp.'

At the reference to his size, Ninety-nine sat up and puffed himself out to look as big as he possibly could, frowning fiercely as he did so, and blowing little showers of sparks with the trickle of smoke that curled from his nostrils.

'I tell you something,' said Ben. 'Talking of size, I do believe he is bigger than when he first landed on my bed. He'd never fit in my pyjama pocket now. How queer!'

It was true. Ninety-nine was the size of a small dog.

'Dragons grow ten times as fast as anything else. I thought everybody knew that,' said Ninety-nine scornfully.

'And look at his flippers!' said Beth. 'They've got a

28

sort of leathery frill along the edge of each one, and I'm sure they weren't there at first. The frills I mean.'

'Frills indeed!' said the little dragon. 'Don't you know sprouting wings when you see them? Wait till they've grown a bit more, then won't I just show you!'

'All the same,' said Father Bell-Wether, 'I still can't believe there can be much danger...'

'Not so much from him,' said Beth, 'but from the ninety-eight dragons who got here first.'

'Ninety-eight dragons!' exclaimed Father Bell-Wether.

'And all of them bigger than me and growing larger every minute!' said Ninety-nine with satisfaction.

'That certainly alters things!' said Father Bell-Wether.

'But where can they all be?' said Ben. 'We haven't seen a trace of them.'

'Did they jump over the same green gate from the Other Side?' asked the ram. Ben shook his head.

'No,' he said. 'It was all my fault, I'm afraid. You see, I counted dragons because I think sheep are s –' He was just going to say 'soppy' when Beth in her turn dug him hard in the ribs with her elbow, and he stopped just in time.

'I mean,' he went on, 'I thought dragons would . . . well . . . make a change.'

'They certainly do,' said Father Bell-Wether drily. 'This is an awkward business. It is our work to help the sleepless to sleep. How do you think they can dream calmly and happily if you start bringing such things Over-the-Gate? Fire-breathing, scaly creatures!'

Ben hung his head unhappily.

'And all the time you are talking about it they are growing bigger and scalier and fierier!' said Ninety-nine. 'Well look at me!'

There was now no doubt at all that he had grown much bigger in the short time the children had known him.

'But if the other ninety-eight jumped over a different gate, they will be in a different part of the country,' said Father Bell-Wether. 'They might be anywhere. There is a second plain, very like this one, separated from us by an impassable ravine. There is a steep track leading down to the bottom from this side, luckily for us, for there is a stream flowing at the bottom, but not even the most agile mountain goat could climb up the other side. That may well be where the dragons are.'

'Don't you know anything about the plain on the other side?' asked Ben.

'Only that there red flowers seem to grow as freely as blue ones grow here, which doesn't seem much help.' He sighed thoughtfully.

'I'm not so sure about that!' said Beth. 'Little red flowers, Ben! Don't you see!'

'There you go again!' said Ben crossly. 'You and your flowers!' Beth said nothing, but stood deep in thought. 'Well, if the ravine is impassable, and the dragons are the other side, I suppose we are safe,' said Ben.

'Until their wings have grown! And they can fly across the ravine,' said Ninety-nine, turning to gaze with satisfaction at his own wings. Ben looked at him sharply. Had they grown even more since he last looked at them? He was not quite sure. The little dragon was lashing his tail and grinning with flicking tongue in the sly way that he remembered. 'And when they've grown,' went on Ninety-nine in a singsong voice, 'the dragons will rise in a great dark cloud with a beating of wings and a trail of sparks flying behind them, and each will circle over the sheep or lamb of its choice, and swoop down and carry off its dinner!'

'Except you!' Ben reminded him.

'You promised!' said Beth.

Ninety-nine stopped lashing his tail.

'Except me!' he said with a sigh.

Father Bell-Wether lifted his great head.

'Clearly we must act before their wings have time to grow,' he said, and there was now no doubt in Ben's mind that the little dragon was bigger. He was the size of a fairy-cycle, and his wings were already wider and less frilly.

'We must work out a plan as quickly as possible,' went on Father Bell-Wether. 'It is not the big and strong who always win, so think as you have never, never thought before!'

# 5. The First Dragon

They sat on the grass and thought so hard that it almost hurt: all except Ninety-nine who leaned with his nobbly back against the rock, his front paws clasped over his scaly yellow chest, doing smoke exercises through his nose. Sometimes the smoke spurted out of one nostril, sometimes the other, now and then both together. Once he managed a smoky spiral, and from time to time he would exclaim: 'Oh, that was a good one!' or 'Did you see that? A smashing corkscrew!' But to his annoyance neither Beth nor Ben took any notice.

He was staring up after a fast vanishing smoke ring through which he had managed to blow a tiny flurry of sparks, when he suddenly gave Ben a nudge with a scaly elbow.

'Oh, do shut up!' said Ben. 'I don't care a hoot about smoke rings. I'd nearly got an idea, and now it's gone!'

Ninety-nine sighed gustily and nudged Beth with the other elbow.

'Ow, that hurt!' she said crossly. 'I wish you wouldn't keep interrupting my thinkings!'

'All right,' said the dragon in an offended voice. 'Don't say I didn't try to tell you.'

'Tell us what?' asked Ben absently.

'Oh, nothing,' said Ninety-nine sulkily. 'I'm only the smallest dragon of all. What I think of things doesn't matter. And you didn't even see my smoke rings and my curlicue!'

Beth turned and looked at his scowling face.

'I'm sorry,' she said. 'I'd love to see them another time, and of course we want to know what you think about things.'

'Well, then,' said Ninety-nine more graciously, 'I think you'd better look there!' With a pointed claw he made jerky stabbing movements up into the sky.

They looked up. Far away in the distance, over the other side of the ravine, was a small black shape, no bigger than a bluebottle, flying in an uncertain way, now high, now low, and as the shape flew nearer, and grew larger, they saw that it was beating the air with large leathery wings.

'The first of the flying dragons!' said Father Bell-Wether.

'Oh, whatever shall we do?' said Beth. 'Suppose it carries off one of the sheep?'

'Not likely!' said Ninety-nine. 'Not that my opinion matters though.'

He tossed his head.

He had picked up a piece of loose sheep's wool lying on the grass and was polishing his claws with it in an off-hand way.

'Oh, come off it, Ninety-nine!' said Ben. 'You know perfectly well we want to know why you think it's not likely!'

Ninety-nine smiled graciously and admired his shining green talons for a minute, then he said:

'It couldn't carry a sheep because it hasn't learned to fly

properly yet. All over the place it is, just look at it! It couldn't manage to carry a lambkin and keep airborne, let alone a sheep. I bet I do better than that when my wings grow big enough.'

'Well, then, what do you think it has come for?' asked Ben.

The flying dragon was above them now, swooping in a jerky way in a wide circle over the plain.

Ninety-nine started to wave, thought better of it, and smirked guiltily. 'Spying out the land, I should think,' he said.

'And all my unsuspecting flock below him as clear as peas on a plate!' said Father Bell-Wether.

Ben looked anxiously round. There was not an inch of cover on the mountainside or the plain below. Nothing but flower-studded grass stretching away as far as the eye could see.

'If you take my advice you'll do something pretty quick. In no time at all the other ninety-seven will be flying over too. I'm told this flying business is as easy as kiss your talons, once your wings have grown and you've had a bit of practice!' Ninety-nine glanced in a self-satisfied way at his own rapidly growing wings. 'He's getting better at it even now!' He nodded at the dragon who, having circled the plain, was flying back the way he had come.

'It isn't wobbling about nearly as much!' said Beth. 'Isn't there anywhere we can hide the sheep?' she said anxiously.

'The only place I can think of,' said Father Bell-Wether, 'is at the bottom of the ravine: it is the best we can do. At least they won't be a sitting target as they are on the mountainside, but even there they may be discovered in the end. But we are wasting valuable time. I must sound the alarm!'

As he spoke he leapt to the top of the rock once more, and at the agitated clanging of his bell the browsing sheep looked up, and with anxious bleating and calling to their lambs, came galloping to the summons.

When at last Father Bell-Wether could make himself heard he lifted his great head and called in his deep voice:

'My children, we are in great danger! There is no time to explain why at this moment, but do as I tell you without question and all may yet be well.'

There were agitated cries of 'Da-anger! Da-a-anger!' and 'Trust Father Bell-Wether!' from the flock, and again the great ram had to sound his bell before he could go on speaking.

'We must go in an orderly fashion, as fast as we can to the track leading down the cliff. I will lead the way. When we reach the stream at the bottom, for a time at least we shall be safe, and there I will tell you more! But wait. Someone must stay at the top of the cliff as sentry. Let me see. Perhaps two sentries would be better. You, Nibbler and Noggins . . .' He was interrupted by an old mother sheep.

'Not my two little sons! Why they are barely grown from lambhood! I am an old sheep with a wise head between my ears. Father, let me stay behind instead!'

'And what chance do you think your fat sides would have of hiding in the shadow of the rock at the top of the path?' said the ram. 'I have chosen them for the very reason that they are small. Are you willing to do this for the sake of the flock, Nibbler and Noggins? You are sensible youngsters.'

'We will guard the path to the last tuft of wool!' said the two young sheep proudly.

'Oh, do hurry up and hide!' said Beth. 'Ben and I will explain what the danger is to the sentries, if you'll only go!'

'You are right,' said Father Bell-Wether, turning to the flock. 'Follow me!'

Before he had finished speaking the sheep were scampering down the mountainside. Ben and Beth ran after them, with Nibbler and Noggins on either side, and as they ran they explained to them about the rapidly growing dragons and what the danger was they must look for. The young sheep skipped and gambolled with excitement and pride at the importance of their task.

'At the first sight of another dragon one of us will leap down the cliff path and warn Father Bell-Wether!' said Nibbler.

'And the other will sta-a-y behind and see what happens next!' said Noggins.

Ben and Beth followed in the wake of the sheep's bobbing white backs. At first they were afraid that they would not be able to keep up with them, but they found themselves moving with the same dream-like swooping movement with which they had come up the mountainside, their bare feet barely seeming to touch the ground. This time, Ninety-nine didn't once say 'Wait for me!' as he had done on the way up. Ben noticed that he lolloped along beside them without any difficulty at all. When at last they all three reached the cliff the two children lay on their stomachs and peered over the edge, between the two sentries. The track certainly was steep, in some places almost sheer, and Beth couldn't help wondering if it wasn't altogether too difficult for human feet. They could see far below where the first of the sheep had already reached the bottom of the ravine, and were clustered round Father Bell-Wether beside the stream, while the rest poured down the track like a white woolly waterfall.

'I don't much fancy climbing down there!' said Ben.

'Nor me!' said Beth.

It was Ninety-nine who put them both to shame by saying:

'Come on, what are we waiting for?'

At the same time he plunged down the track, and after only a brief pause Ben and Beth followed him. They neither of them dared to look down to the bottom again, but having started to clamber down so fearfully, where there seemed to be no foothold, as Ben said later, they seemed 'almost to bounce in slow motion from one sticking out rock to another'. As for Ninety-nine, he led the way with a series of 'Whoops!', clapping his flippers as he leapt from stone to stone. At the tail end of the woolly cascade of animals was the old sheep with her two lambs, Mortimer and Matilda, who both kept looking over their shoulders at Ninety-nine with a good deal of interest. Once or twice Mortimer tried to say 'Whoops!' instead of 'Baa!' Ninety-nine looked rather pleased.

When they arrived at the bottom at last, Beth and Ben heaved a sigh of relief. The strange light that on the plain above seemed clearer than moonlight but softer than sunlight, down here was dim and mysterious. The stream gushed from the rock in two separate rivulets which joined together and flowed chuckling and clucking down the ravine. The ground near the bank was boggy. Ninety-nine wrinkled his nose in disgust and leapt on to a dry rock.

'Dragons do not like getting their feet wet!' he said crossly, shaking each paw in turn like a cat. But nobody was listening, except Mortimer and Matilda who jumped up beside him, shaking each small hoof in turn in imitation, though they were not quite sure what for. Beth had

flopped down on the bank, and from her cupped hands she was just about to drink some water from the stream, when Ben called out:

'Don't be an ass! Don't drink it!' For he felt that anything might happen in this strange place.

'I must,' said Beth unexpectedly. 'It's the only way of finding out for certain!'

'Finding out what?' asked Ben. But Beth was already drinking.

'I thought as much!' she said, when she had done wiping her wet hands on her nightdress.

'What are you talking about?' said Ben crossly.

'Drink some of the stream and I think you'll see,' said Beth. Rather reluctantly Ben knelt down beside her and drank too.

'That's queer,' he said. 'It isn't quite like plain water. It tastes . . .' He paused and licked his lips thoughtfully, and then he said, 'It tastes of toothpaste!'

Beth nodded. '*Now* do you see?' she said.

'I think I'm beginning to!' he said slowly.

# 6. The Ravine

'In some queer way,' said Ben, 'this Over-the-Gate country is like our own bedroom – but gone wild and strange – and . . . and huge. Or else we've become very small. Could be either.'

Beth nodded. 'The sheep side with the blue flowers is like my bed.'

'And the dragon side with red flowers is like mine,' said Ben.

'And the floor between,' Beth interrupted, 'is the ravine, and the stream starts from two places because we upset two tooth mugs of water, and that explains why the stream tastes of tooth-paste! But I don't understand why there's a great mountain on my side.'

'Easy,' said Ben. 'Your great hulking knees sticking up. You always sleep like that, lying on your back. That's why you snore.'

'I don't snore!' said Beth indignantly.

'You do!'

'I don't!'

'Oh, don't let's argue now!' said Ben.

'Well, if you're so clever, why is there a path down my side of the cliff, and not on yours?' went on Beth.

'Because your bedspread was trailing on the floor,' said Ben. 'I saw it after Dad had gone and you were flopping about because you still couldn't go to sleep. I'm glad we've worked all this out. It makes me feel more comfortable inside somehow.'

'All the same,' said Beth. 'Dragons aren't very comfortable to have around, not ninety-eight big ones.'

While they were talking, Father Bell-Wether had been explaining their danger to his anxious flock.

'Just look at Ninety-nine!' whispered Ben.

Mortimer and Matilda were paying no attention to Father Bell-Wether. They were watching the little dragon, who was now the size of a grown-up bicycle. He was jumping off his rock, with a 'Whoops!' and flapping his half-grown wings to test their strength. After several jumps it seemed to Ben that at last they gave him a tiny lift. It was quite clear that he was well aware of the admiring gaze of the lambs. In a condescending way he explained to them how he did it.

'Simple!' he said. 'Flatten out your wings when you take off and flap like mad!'

Several lambs, including Mortimer and Matilda, began jumping off rocks and saying 'Whoops!' and thrashing their tails from side to side in the best imitation of flapping wings they could manage. The older sheep huddled uneasily in the shadow of the cliff, their fears only half soothed by their leader explaining that for the time being they were safe.

'Please,' said Ben to Father Bell-Wether, 'what generally happens when you jump over the gate and land this side? I mean what do you do?'

'We feed and rest to regain our strength ready to jump over the next gate.'

'How do you know when that's going to be?' asked Beth.

'We don't know,' said Father Bell-Wether. 'It all depends on the first Sleeper. First the light grows lighter, just before he begins to stir before waking. Then we know we must be ready to be counted again by someone else while we jump yet again over another gate; someone else who can't go to sleep. We have a busy time of it, I can tell you! It's jump! Jump! Jump! As soon as you are waking in England and there's no longer need for us here, there will be people in Australia, or Japan, or New Zealand or somewhere, who can't sleep, and counting jumping sheep to send themselves off, just as you did. It's a hard life! And never so much as a thank-you. But we don't complain. What would the poor things do without us?'

There were 'baa's' of agreement, and much sober head-nodding among the older sheep at this.

'Then if we keep the dragons off until you can escape over another gate the sheep will be safe?' said Beth.

'That is so,' said the ram, 'and remember the light grows lighter just before this happens. But if the dragons find the ravine with the stream at the bottom before then, we shall be discovered. They will need to drink just as we do.'

'And eat!' interrupted Ninety-nine. 'You can't expect dragons to live on grass, like a lot of sheep. What they like to eat for dinner is . . .'

Nobody doubted what the last word was going to be, but nobody actually heard it because he was interrupted by an agitated bleating and a shower of small stones from half-way down the cliff path. There were cries of 'Nibbler!' and 'The look-out lamb!' and 'News! News!' from the sheep who were gazing anxiously upwards.

'And bad news by the look of it!' said Ben.

The young sheep leapt from rock to rock down the lower slopes of the mountain and galloped panting up to Father Bell-Wether.

'Dragons!' he cried. 'Dragons! Hundreds of them! Flying towards the ravine in a great, black, wing-flapping cloud!'

'Not hundreds!' said Father Bell-Wether crisply. 'Don't exaggerate, my dear Nibbler. There can't be more than ninety-eight, though that's bad enough!'

'What shall we do? What shall we do?' bleated the terrified sheep.

'Stop bleating to begin with,' said Father Bell-Wether, 'or we shall be discovered at once, but if that happens your hooves are sharp, so fight! For the sake of your lambs!'

'But I don't think it need come to that,' said Ben suddenly. 'I think I know another, safer hiding place.'

'You do? But where?' said Father Bell-Wether in surprise.

'I'm pretty sure there is a cave under the cliff if we can only find the entrance,' said Ben. 'Stay where you are while Beth and I try to find it!'

Beth was looking at her brother in astonishment. 'Whatever are you talking about?' she said.

'Don't you see!' said Ben. 'That great empty space under your bed. I bet it's turned into a sort of cave!

There's probably one on the other side of the ravine too. Come on and help me look for it, instead of standing there gawping! Somewhere near the source of the stream we should find it, where your bedspread began to trail on the floor!'

Ben and Beth hurried up the ravine, stumbling over rocks and squelching through boggy places, and as they went they examined the side of the cliff, watched all the time with barely stifled bleats of anxiety by the waiting sheep. Father Bell-Wether followed close behind. Sure enough, they found it at last. Hidden beneath a trail of blue-flowered creeper was a tall triangular opening which led into a great high cave.

'Quick!' said Ben, holding the creeper aside. 'In with you, before the dragons spy the ravine and come down to drink!'

'Follow me!' said Father Bell-Wether. 'And not a single bleat! The lives of your lambs may depend upon it!'

There were one or two quickly stifled 'Baa's', and the flock of sheep poured after their leader into the dark cave.

When Ninety-nine tried to follow, after the last woolly back had disappeared into the darkness, Beth just caught him by his scaly pointed tail. He twitched it indignantly away.

'I shall stand just inside the opening and mount guard!' he said coldly. 'How do you think poor old Bell-Wether can manage that silly lot all by himself?

'Well, don't forget your promise!' said Beth.

'I have made a solemn dragon oath,' said Ninety-nine

indignantly. 'Are you suggesting that I would harm my friends Mortimer and Matilda? I should like to see anyone try!' He sat up on his hind legs, clenched his front claws and blew a shower of sparks through his nose, then he dropped on his paws again and disappeared into the cave.

Ben and Beth rearranged the creeper over the entrance so that not a trace of it could be seen. A horrid thought suddenly came into Ben's mind. He pulled the creeper aside a mere crack and whispered:

'I say, Ninety-nine, are you there? Do dragons like to eat . . .? I mean to say, I suppose they don't . . .'

'Eat boys and girls?' Ninety-nine whispered back. 'Not likely. Too tough.'

The two children breathed a sigh of relief and readjusted the creeper once more. They were not a moment too soon.

# 7. To the Rescue

As Beth was replacing the last strand, Ben said suddenly:
'Listen, what's that?'

'What's what?' asked Beth. 'There's only the noise of
the stream – and me humming.'

'I don't mean that,' said Ben impatiently. 'A sort
of flapping noise, like a lot of people beating a lot of
carpets!'

Beth listened, and her startled face showed that she
heard it too. The beating noise grew louder and nearer
until it seemed to merge into a great roar. It was so loud
that they both put their hands over their ears. At the same
time the light grew suddenly dim. They looked up to the
space between the top of the two cliffs, where the strip of
sky seemed to wind above them as the stream wound
down the ravine at their feet. A great black cloud was
blocking out the daylight.

Ben pulled Beth's hands from her ears and shouted:
'The dragons! Here they come!'

For a few seconds the sky was completely blotted out,
but gradually the thunder of beating wings became
quieter and faded into the distance, and the sky was clear
once more.

'Phew!' said Beth. 'What a mercy we got the sheep into
the cave in time! When they can't find anything but grass
and flowers on this side perhaps they'll just fly back again.

I don't suppose they spotted the ravine, they were flying so fast.'

'We don't know what they spotted,' said Ben. 'Did you see their great eyes? As big and yellow as traffic lights they were.' He paused for a minute and then went on uneasily, 'Wait a minute, though! You said there was nothing up there this side but grass and flowers. What about Noggins?'

'The other look-out lamb?' said Beth. 'I'd forgotten all about him! Oh, poor little thing, we can't leave him up there all by himself!'

'He won't be by himself,' said Ben gloomily. 'He'll be with ninety-eight dragons.'

'Whatever shall we do?' said Beth.

'There's only one thing we can do,' said Ben. 'Climb up the cliff path again and find out what's happening.'

'Oh!' said Beth unhappily. She remembered the sound of the beating of the dragons' wings, and their great shining yellow eyes: not to mention the steepness of the track they had just climbed down. 'Do we have to?'

'Of course we have to,' said Ben. 'Come on! I know what you're thinking, but Ninety-nine said: "Not likely, too tough!" and he's a dragon too so he's sure to know.'

Ben spoke jerkily. He had already started to climb, and his voice grew fainter as he clambered higher and higher up the track, urging Beth to hurry as he did so.

Beth was not quite sure if she began climbing because she did not like the idea of being left behind, or because she remembered how very small the look-out lamb had been, and how brave it was of him to stay by himself at the top of the cliff. Whichever it was, climb she did. This time, instead of the easy floating movement with which they had swooped up the mountainside and over the grassy plain, her feet felt as heavy as lead, as she said to Ben afterwards, as though all her not-wanting-to had sunk down inside them and was trying to hold her back. But she struggled gallantly on, saying from time to time: 'Not likely! Too tough!' to keep up her spirits.

On she clambered, pulling herself up from one boulder to another, her nightdress clinging round her knees in a discouraging way, her heavy, reluctant feet, feeling for the next foothold. She thought she would never get to the top. Just as she thought she could not go one step farther, the rock she was standing on gave way and went rattling down the cliff beneath her with a shower of small stones, and she was left holding on by her hands to an over-hanging rock, her feet kicking wildly.

'Help!' she shouted, and a voice just above her replied in a hoarse whisper:

'Shut up, you silly owl! Don't make a row!'

It was Ben, and she was so pleased to see him peering down at her over the edge of the rock to which she was clinging, that she forgot to mind being called a silly owl. She only felt relief at the warm grip of his hands round her weakening wrists.

'It's all right. I've got you. I'm on a sort of stone plat-form, just below the top. But for goodness' sake don't make a noise. I think I can hear the dragons! They can't be far away. Put your right foot on that rock, and your other knee on this one here and you can easily get back on the path again.'

Slowly and painfully Beth pulled herself up and flopped
panting beside Ben. He watched her anxiously.

'Are you all right?'

Beth nodded. She was too out of breath to speak.

'Whew!' he said. 'That was a pretty massive climb.
You didn't do it half badly.'

Beth went quite pink at such unexpected praise.

'What do we do now?' she whispered when she had got her breath back again. 'The look-out post was just above us, wasn't it?'

Ben nodded.

'Noggins!' he called in a low voice. 'Are you there? It's us, Beth and Ben, the two humans! I say, Noggins!'

There was no reply from the look-out lamb, but they could hear something else, a strange, distant gritty, grating, grumbling noise, like a whole fleet of cement-mixers all grinding together, now loud, now soft.

'I don't like it,' said Beth firmly. 'That noise I mean, whatever it is.'

'Nor do I,' said Ben. 'But there's nothing else for it, noise or no, we shall have to go and look for Noggins.'

'Supposing –' began Beth.

'Don't let's stop to suppose anything,' said Ben, 'or we might get too scared to go on. I'll wriggle over the top and then give you a hand, but whatever you do, keep your head down. Once we're up, if we lie flat on our stomachs the grass should be long enough to hide us.'

# 8. Poor Noggins!

They scrambled over the ledge on to the plain above them and lay side by side on the ground. The gritty grumbling noise was louder now. They parted the long grass cautiously and peered through, but in the small space that this opened up there was no sign of Noggins.

'If we wriggle on our stomachs as far as the shadow of the rock, where the look-out was, we could sit up and perhaps see a bit more without being seen,' said Ben. 'Come on!'

They worked their way steadily through the long grass, the strange noise growing louder all the time, until at last they reached the shadow of the rock, then they sat up cautiously. There was still no sign of Noggins. Only a few wisps of wool showed where the two lambs had waited. Anxiously they peered round the rock.

Not far away, at the bottom of the slope which fell gently away below them, they looked down on a strange sight. It was the dragons, all ninety-eight of them. They were drawn up in a circle in order of size, from the largest, who was as big as a bus, to the smallest, who was the size of a milk-cart, their pointed tails lying on the grass behind them like the spokes of a wheel. Their leathery wings were folded, and Ben and Beth could see that they were as green as parsley on top, and as yellow as scrambled egg underneath, with a row of nobbles down the back, just as

Ben remembered them, but much, much bigger. There was no doubt what the gritty grumbling noise was. It was their angry arguing voices.

'And I say it's a shame! Telling us there were sheep all over the place here, ready for the snatching,' rumbled one of the dragons. 'And all there is is one measly little lamb. A couple of mouthfuls of wool and no more!' said another.

'If that's Eleven's idea of a joke it isn't mine!' said a third. 'All that hard work jumping over that enormous high gate. I tell you . . .'

But here the dragon the children guessed must be Eleven interrupted.

'*I* keep telling you, but you won't believe me!' he said. 'By my two yellow eyes, I swear I saw them! They were all over the plain and the mountainside.'

'That must be the first flying dragon!' whispered Ben. Beth nodded.

'The one who came to spy out the land. They've got him in the middle of the circle . . . and Ben!' she went on.

'Look! He's got Noggins beside him. He's hiding his eyes with his front hooves, and his tail is all droopy, and no wonder, surrounded by all those great creatures. Oh, poor little Noggins! He looks so frightened.' And without thinking she jumped up and shouted: 'Noggins! Noggins! It's all right! We're here!'

Her shrill voice could be heard even above the rumbling, grumbling of the dragons, which stopped abruptly.

'Now you've done it!' said Ben. And 'done it' she certainly had. All ninety-eight of them turned to see where the voice came from, as though every long green nose had been pulled by a string.

There was a moment of astonished silence, in which Noggins gave a tiny relieved bleat in reply, and then the largest dragon rumbled: 'A man-child and a girl-child, by my pointed tail!' and followed by all the others he started to lumber up the little hill towards them.

Ben had joined Beth, and she felt for his hand. 'It's all right,' he said. 'Don't panic. Remember, "Not likely, too tough!"' But he seemed quite glad to have his hand held all the same. As the dragons came nearer the children worked their way to the top of the rock, facing forward all the time. Here they felt a little safer.

'Oh dear,' said Beth. 'I wish Ninety-nine was here. I'm sure he'd help us. But it's no good wishing when he's inside the cave at the bottom of the ravine . . . unless . . . Ben, could you whistle for him, like you did before? Do you think he'd hear?'

'I can try. We can't attract more attention than we have already,' said Ben gloomily. He eyed the dragons uneasily. They had nearly reached the foot of the rock.

'Go on, whistle!' said Beth.

Ben put two fingers between his lips and whistled loudly and rather desperately, the dragons halted in surprise.

'Why did you do that?' asked the largest dragon suspiciously. 'I never did trust humans since that business with St George. Well, why did you do it?'

'It's . . . well, it's . . . it's just a noise that humans make sometimes,' said Ben in reply, adding wildly: 'Just as – cocks crow . . . and cows moo, and . . . and dragons make

gritty grumbling noises. It's quite easy. You put two fingers in your mouth and blow, like this.' And he gave an even shriller, louder whistle.

'If only Noggins will have the sense to run away,' whispered Beth. 'They've forgotten all about him and left him behind.'

Several dragons put a couple of claws in their scaly mouths and blew, making the strangest noise. It sounded rather like the hooting of impatient cars in a very large traffic jam. None of them produced anything like a whistle.

'Keep their attention somehow,' whispered Beth. 'Noggins is running away!'

'No, no, you haven't got it right,' called Ben to the dragons, and he whistled a third time, while with relief he watched the little lamb growing smaller and smaller in the distance.

Once more the great creatures tried, but with no more success than before.

'Again!' commanded the dragons. 'Do it again, man-child!'

Now whistling down your fingers is not easy, and Ben had only just learned how to do it. He knew it didn't work every time. He put his fingers in his mouth and blew a fourth time, but no sound came. The dragons began to mutter among themselves.

'Well, why don't you do it?' grumbled the largest dragon, and as Ben tried unsuccessfully again the grumbling grew to a rumbling.

'Well, anyway, Noggins has escaped,' said Beth. 'But, oh dear, they're getting angry. Whatever shall we do?'

And then above the mounting sound of the grumbling of the dragons they heard the unmistakable sound of flapping leathery wings.

'Look!' said Beth, pointing excitedly. 'It's Ninety-nine. I'm sure it is!'

Both dragons and children looked up. 'Goodness, how he's grown! And he's flying!'

He certainly was flying, but in the same uncertain way as Eleven had done when he came to spy out the land. He circled unsteadily round them, watched by the two children with delight, and the dragons with curiosity, then with leathery wings extended, floated downwards, making a rather wobbly landing in the narrow space between children and dragons, leaving two long scars in the grass where he had braked with his scaly heels.

# 9. The Signal

'What about that for a neat landing?' said Ninety-nine cheerfully, blowing a cloud of smoke and a fountain of rainbow-coloured sparks. He was certainly very much bigger. Almost as large as the dragon who was as big as a milk-cart.

'Ninety-nine!' roared the largest dragon. 'Stop showing off and explain yourself! Where have you been all this time?'

Ninety-nine looked down humbly. 'Where have I been? I . . . well . . . I lost my way. You see the gate was so very, *very* tall, and I was so very, *very* small. The smallest of you all, don't forget. I couldn't jump over it first go,' he went on truthfully, 'and . . . well . . . by the time I managed it, you'd all gone, and I didn't know where to find you. But here I am at last.'

'And we're so glad you've come!' said Beth.

But Ninety-nine, who had not looked in their direction, gave the two children a quick frowning glance, with a shake of the head that was only just noticeable, before turning away again.

'As if I hadn't enough to worry about,' said the largest dragon. 'What with suddenly finding ourselves in this strange place, with nothing to eat or drink, and all of us starving, without you youngsters getting out of hand! There's Eleven here bringing us all the way from the plain with red flowers, with the promise of fat sheep all over the place, and some of the smaller ones barely able to fly a straight course. And what do we find? Nothing except one single, scrawny lamb!'

He turned to where Noggins had been standing, and glared in surprise.

'And bless me, if even that one hasn't disappeared! Eleven!' he roared. 'You might at least have kept an eye on him! I'm so hungry that even that would have been better than nothing.'

The largest dragon turned angrily to tell the unfortunate Eleven what he thought of him, helped by all the other hungry dragons. While their attention was distracted Ninety-nine sidled up to Ben and Beth. 'Don't let on you know me,' he said out of the corner of his mouth. 'It would only make them suspicious. And whatever I do or say, don't interfere. Trust Ninety-nine! It's lucky for you I suddenly realized that if I stayed inside the cave I should pretty soon grow too big to squeeze through the opening again – horrible that would have been – and if I hadn't come outside I should never have heard you whistle . . . Look out! He's coming back.'

When the largest dragon turned round again Ninety-nine was gazing over the plain under the shadow of a scaly paw saying something about 'looking for that ungrateful lamb you mentioned. And talking of lambs, I'm pretty hungry myself.' And then to Ben and Beth's unspeakable horror he went on: 'But I think our troubles are over. You see Eleven was not so far wrong. There are quite a lot of sheep here, about fifty I should say, counting the one that got away.'

'Fifty sheep!' roared the largest dragon in delighted surprise. Beth's horrified, 'Oh, how could you!' was drowned by the joyful whoops of all the other dragons.

'Where are they?' asked the largest dragon, and his pointed tongue flicked in and out in the way that Beth and Ben remembered only too well. The two children could hardly believe their ears when Ninety-nine replied:

'Under your very claws, in a cave beneath the cliff.'

'Well, hurry up and show us the way there,' roared all the dragons together.

'Now be patient and I'll explain!' said Ninety-nine. 'On the way here you flew across a deep ravine.'

'Ah, I think I saw it,' said the largest dragon. 'I remember noticing that all the flowers the other side are red, and this side they are all blue. Funny that.'

'The sheep! The sheep!' grumbled the other dragons. 'Never mind about flowers. We want our dinner!' And all the others took up the cry:

'We want our dinner! We want our dinner!'

'Have patience,' roared Ninety-nine above the din. 'Because we shall have to lollop quite a long way before we find it although the cave is just below us. There is a path down the cliff, but it is far too narrow for such well-grown dragons as we are. But if we fly to the far end of the ravine,' and here Ninety-nine pointed in the opposite direction to the cave, 'then double back, you can quench your thirst at the stream that runs between the two cliffs, then lollop upstream beside it until you come to the cave. We can't fly up the ravine. It's too narrow.' To Beth's fury he added: 'I have pulled the creeper aside so that you can see the way into the cave. You simply can't miss it.'

Unable to restrain herself any longer she hissed: 'How could you! You gave a solemn dragon promise ...'

But before she could say any more, Ninety-nine's pointed tail swished round and hit her sharply on the ankle.

'Ow! That hurt,' said Beth.

'Don't you see, you silly owl,' hissed Ben. 'He told us not to interrupt. He said "Trust Ninety-nine!" and I do. I believe he's got something up his sleeve.'

This time Beth, whose leg was smarting from the dragon's blow, and her feelings from being called 'a silly owl' again so soon, could only think of saying in reply: 'Dragons don't have sleeves!'

While this conversation was going on the largest dragon was getting all the others into line according to their size.

'Come along there! Hurry up! I'm as empty as a balloon and dry as a cinder. No pushing there!' he roared. 'Now then, Ninety-nine, we're ready. Lead the way!'

Ninety-nine gave a bashful smirk and said: 'But you are the largest dragon and the leader of us all, and I am the smallest and least important animal. My place is at the end of the line. You will find the way quite easily if you go first.'

'Oh, wise young Ninety-nine!' said the largest dragon. 'Not only has he found food and drink for his starving brothers, but he has a proper respect for his elders. Mark that, you brothers!'

In no time at all the line was ready: 'Wings raised!' roared the largest dragon. 'Follow me!'

One after another they took off, and the noise of their ninety-eight pairs of leathery wings was as deafening as the beating of ninety-eight carpets at spring-cleaning time, and the wind of their flapping nearly knocked the two children off their feet. Silently they watched the

63

flying column grow smaller and smaller in the sky, their scales flashing green and gold more brightly than they had ever done before, and leaving a trail of smoke and golden sparks behind them. Ninety-nine gave a great gusty sigh.

'Well, that's all right so far, I suppose.'

'All right, you say? But I don't understand,' replied Beth miserably. 'We'd hidden the sheep so safely and helped little Noggins to escape, and now –'

'I can't stop to explain,' said Ninety-nine. 'But do as I tell you! Didn't you notice how their scales flashed in a way you've never seen before? If that doesn't tell you anything I'll explain in a minute. But first of all go to the top of the cliff path and whistle as loud as ever you can! It's a signal to Father Bell-Wether that the coast is clear. Go on, whistle!' he went on impatiently.

Without waiting for any further explanation Ben ran to the edge of the cliff, and putting two fingers in his mouth he whistled. This time it worked, shrill and clear. In the silence that followed there was the faintest answering 'Ba-a-a!' from the bottom of the ravine.

# 10. The Sleeper Wakes

'But I still don't understand,' said Beth unhappily.

'I can't stay long. I must be quick and catch up my dragon brothers or they will suspect something,' said Ninety-nine. 'But I'll explain as shortly as possible. I told you why I came out of the cave?' The two children nodded. 'Well, there I was, mounting guard outside the entrance when I noticed that the light was growing brighter. Even at the bottom of the ravine I could tell. Why, I could count the scales on my left hind leg, and I couldn't do that before. Didn't you notice the light?'

'We were too worried,' said Ben.

'Perhaps that's why the dragons looked so splendid when they flew away,' said Beth. 'All shining green and gold.'

'Well, I told Father Bell-Wether, and he joined me outside the cave and reminded me that it was the first warning sign that the Sleeper was about to wake and that he must get the flock up on to the plain again or he wouldn't be able to find the next gate for the next Sleeper. The cave had served its turn and saved the flock when the dragons flew over the ravine.'

'I think I'm beginning to understand,' said Beth.

'So after some desperate thinking we planned that I should come up here and tell my dragon brothers that the sheep were hiding in the cave. I knew they'd do anything to find them, they'd be so hungry. I'm pretty peckish myself, I don't mind telling you! Now I'm so much bigger my hungriness has grown too. Much more of me to feel hungry.' He clasped his empty yellow stomach with both paws.

'Do go on explaining!' said Beth. 'Never mind your stomach!'

'It's all very well for some!' said Ninety-nine glumly. 'Well, we arranged that I should tell them the longest possible way to the cave, to give the flock time to get safely up the cliff. We were just wondering what sign I could give to tell him the coast was clear and that my brothers were safely out of the way, when we heard you whistle, and that was the answer – that's why I asked you to do it again.'

'But when they find the cave is empty, won't they follow the sheep up here?' said Ben.

'Not up the cliff path, they won't,' said Ninety-nine. 'They're all too large. I couldn't get up myself. I had to fly.'

'Well, won't they fly too?' said Ben obstinately.

'Not a hope!' said Ninety-nine. 'I could only just spread my wings between the two sides of the ravine; the tips were touching in several places. Quite sore they are, and I'm the smallest of them all don't forget!'

'I'm very sorry I was so horrid,' said Beth uncomfortably. 'I mean, accusing you of breaking your word.'

Ninety-nine waved a gracious paw.

'As if I would hurt a single sheep! Hadn't I given my solemn dragon promise? Besides, who would injure Matilda and Mortimer and their little friends? So trusting as they are! Besides I must admit it is pleasant to be admired. I tell you, I left those lambs trying to blow coloured sparks because they enjoyed my performance so!' He smirked in a self-satisfied way. 'But listen, what's that?'

In the silence that followed, far away down the ravine they heard the ringing of a bell.

'Father Bell-Wether!' said Ninety-nine, and they all three rushed to the edge of the cliff and looked over. Hurrying up the steep path was the great ram followed by his flock. Already they were half-way up the path. Mortimer and Matilda at the end leaping gallantly from rock to rock.

'Look at the ravine at the bottom!' said Ben.

On either side of the stream flowed a river of green knobbly backs with pointed tails trailing behind, moving steadily up the valley towards the cave.

'The dragons!' said Beth and Ben together.

On lumbered the great creatures, pushing and jostling up the narrow way, their wings crowded to their sides, grunting and grumbling as they went.

'Oh, dear!' said Ninety-nine. 'I'd forgotten it was so boggy. They will be cross at getting their feet wet!'

As he spoke, Father Bell-Wether reached the top of the path and leapt up on to the plain, the flock of sheep streaming after him. At once they settled peacefully down to crop the soft grass as though they had never heard of dragons. The children's joyful welcome was suddenly interrupted by a muffled roar from the bottom of the ravine. Ninety-nine nodded. 'They've discovered that the cave is empty and the sheep are gone.'

'All that smoke they are snorting makes it difficult to

see what's happening, and all those red sparks!' said Beth who was looking over the edge again.

'Red sparks?' said Ninety-nine. 'That means they're angry! Hallo, they've spotted the last of the sheep climbing up the path!'

Ninety-eight pairs of yellow eyes stared up through the smoke at the tail end of the flock which was just reaching the top of the cliff, and another roar shook the walls of the ravine.

'Come on, Mortimer! Hurry up, Matilda!' called Ninety-nine hoarsely to the two lambs who were at the end of the file, and as he spoke they leapt to the safety of the plain.

'What are the dragons doing now?' asked Beth anxiously. 'I still can't see properly!' The roar had settled down to a steady rumbling, grumbling.

'Turning back to lollop down the ravine the way they came, by the sound of it,' said Ninety-nine.

'But won't your brothers be very angry with you, when they find out you've tricked them?'

'They won't know,' said Ninety-nine simply. 'And I certainly shan't tell them! That's why I must join them before they miss me.'

'I feel quite sorry for them,' went on Beth. 'Being so very hungry. What will you do?'

'Why, go home of course,' said Ninety-nine. 'Back where we came from.'

'Where's that?' asked Ben with interest, but he didn't hear the dragon's reply because of the sudden sharp ringing of Father Bell-Wether's bell. The old ram was standing with head raised, looking restlessly about him.

'The light grows brighter still!' he called. 'Do not go farther than baaing distance, my children. Any moment the Sleeper may awake!'

The light shone harshly now, on his up-flung head and great curling horns. It picked out with startling clearness each blue flower and every blade of grass, and the soft fleeces of the sheep. The only ones not grazing were Mortimer and Matilda, and a number of the smaller lambs who stood in a ring round Ninety-nine, gazing up at him with admiring eyes. He smiled graciously down at them, and patted the nearest of them on the head with a scaly paw and said graciously:

'Well climbed, little lambkins! Well climbed!'

Then as the light grew almost unbearably bright, Father Bell-Wether called urgently:

'To your places, my children! To your places! It is nearly time!'

At once the flock ceased grazing, and with much baaing

and some jostling formed a long line behind him, and as they did so it seemed to the children the scene began to shift and shiver, as a reflection in still water does when it is disturbed by the falling of a stone.

'The Sleeper stirs in his dreams!' said Father Bell-Wether. 'We must go in search of the gate of the next Sleeper. Did I not tell you that it isn't always the big and strong who win! Good-bye, humans, and thank you,' he went on. 'But next time, do not make it dragons! Remember this is sheep country!'

'I won't forget!' called Ben. 'Good-bye.'

The ram's voice and the chorus of baas that accompanied it grew fainter as he led the line of sheep away into the swirling scene before the children. 'Good-bye! Good-bye!' they both called. Now even the ground round their feet seemed to stir and dimple.

'I must go too and find my brothers!' said Ninety-nine.

As he spoke he clapped his great leathery wings together, and with a deep-throated but unmistakable 'Whoops!' he rose into the air.

Ben and Beth watched him spiral steeply above them, a splendid, fully-grown young dragon.

'Good-bye!' he called.

'Good-bye!' called Ben and Beth.

The light shone so brightly on his gleaming emerald scales that they were both dazzled. They felt for each other's hands and closed their eyes. The bleating of the sheep had faded into silence. The only sound was the regular beating of the dragon's wings which instead of fading away grew faster and sharper, until it began to sound not like the beat of leathery wings but the knocking of someone on wood, and a familiar voice called out:

'Wake up, children! Time to get up! I'm afraid we're rather late this morning.' It was their mother knocking on the bedroom door.

They both opened their eyes with a jerk. Ben was in his own familiar bed with the red flowery bedspread, and Beth was in hers with the blue flowers. Slowly they both sat up, and the bedspreads swirled and dimpled as they did so, and then were still.

Ben gave a mighty yawn.

'I've had such a funny dream,' he said.

'So have I,' said Beth. 'Mine was about sheep and lambs with black stockings,' she went on, expecting Ben to laugh at her. But he didn't.

'And dragons too?' he asked.

Beth nodded, and began to pour out the whole strange story.

'You needn't go on,' said Ben. 'I know all about it. I was there too. But we'd better buck up and get dressed or we shall be late for school.'

'I suppose it must have been a dream,' he said just before they went downstairs. 'But it's a funny thing. I've never heard of two people having the same dream before.' And he slid down the banisters all ready for breakfast.

That is the strange story of the ninety-nine dragons. Next time you can't go to sleep and start counting sheep jumping over a gate, if some of them say 'Whoops!' instead of 'Baaaa!' you'll know the reason why.

# About the Author

Barbara Sleigh was born in 1906 in Warwickshire. Her father was an artist, and as a child she spent a great deal of time messing about in his studio. While he worked he told her endless stories.

She was educated at St Catherine's School, Bramley, and later went to an art school. She took an art teacher's training and taught both boys and girls in the Black Country. At about this time she began to write stories for children for that new-fangled thing, radio. She was a lecturer at Goldsmiths' College, then in 1933 she joined the staff of B.B.C. Children's Hour and three years later married David Davis, who was later to become Head of Children's Hour.

As well as writing plays and stories for radio, Barbara Sleigh began writing books in 1955. *Carbonel*, *Kingdom of Carbonel*, *Carbonel and Calidor* and *Grimblegraw and the Wuthering Witch* are published in Puffin. Barbara Sleigh died in 1982.

## THE FURTHER ADVENTURES OF GOBBOLINO AND THE LITTLE WOODEN HORSE
*Ursula Moray Williams*

It nearly broke Gobbolino's heart to have to leave his new, comfortable life as a kitchen cat, but his sister Sootica was in trouble and he had to help her. The road to Hurricane Mountains took Gobbolino and his steadfast friend, the little wooden horse, through many exciting and magical adventures – sometimes so dangerous that neither of them could be sure they would ever see home again!

## TREEHORN'S TREASURE
*Florence Parry Heide*

Treehorn was sitting under a tree in the garden, reading a book, when he happened to glance up and see that the leaves on the tree were turning into dollar bills! But no one would listen when he tried to share his discovery. What was he to do? A hugely entertaining story for 6 to 8-year-olds.

## PROFESSOR BRANESTAWM'S MOUSE WAR
*Norman Hunter*

Take an unwanted mouse – and a much-needed house – and you have two more tricky problems for the inimitable Professor Branestawm! As ever, his instant solution to any problem is to invent another of his incredible machines, but they never seem to behave quite as he intended – sometimes with catastrophic results.

## ONCE UPON A RHYME

*Sara and Stephen Corrin*

From skyscrapers to Guy Fawkes, ducks on a pond to rosebuds, and pirates to man-eating alligators: Sara and Stephen Corrin, so well known for their collections of stories for children, have put the spontaneous relish back into young children's poetry reading with this delicious selection of poems young children will really enjoy.

## DINNER LADIES DON'T COUNT

*Bernard Ashley*

Two children, two problems and trouble at school. Jason storms around the school in a temper and then gets the blame for something he didn't do. Linda tells a lie, just a little one – and is horrified to see how big it grows. Just as it seems that things can't get worse, help comes for each of them in surprising ways.

## YOUNG PUFFIN CROSSWORDS

*Mavis Cavendish*

A step-by-step approach to crossword puzzles that are both informative and the greatest fun to do. For 6 to 8-year-olds.

## HIGGLETY, PIGGLETY, POP!

*Maurice Sendak*

The gloriously fantastical adventures of Jennie, the Sealyham terrier, who leaves her home in search of her heart's desire. A strange and wonderful story which is certain to enjoy as much popularity as *Where the Wild Things Are*.

## THE PERFECT HAMBURGER

*Alexander McCall Smith*

If only Joe could remember *exactly* what he had thrown so haphazardly into the mixing-bowl, he knew that his perfect hamburger could revive his friend Mr Borthwick's ailing business and drive every other fast-food store off the High Street. A grand opening announcing the perfect hamburger is arranged – but will Joe and Mr Borthwick find the vital ingredient in time?

## RAGDOLLY ANNA

*Jean Kenward*

Although she's only made from a morsel of this and a tatter of that, Ragdolly Anna is a very special doll. And within hours of beginning to live with the Little Dressmaker, the White Cat and Dummy, she embarks on some hair-raising adventures.

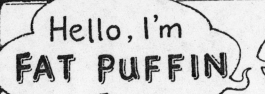